. . . girls flap

their hair

hot lipstick gloss

and candy hairspray

sticks to the air

they scream

they sing

the dahk-dahk of darts

and a thousand ant people

down below

Juan Felipe Herrera

Cinnamon
Girl

letters found inside
a cereal box

HARPER TEEN
An Imprint of HarperCollinsPublishers

HarperTeen is an imprint of HarperCollins Publishers.

Cinnamon Girl: Letters Found Inside a Cereal Box

Library of Congress Cataloging-in-Publication Data
Herrera, Juan Felipe.
  Cinnamon girl : letters found inside a cereal box / Juan Felipe Herrera.—1st ed.
    p.   cm.
  "Joanna Cotler Books."
  Summary: Yolanda, a Puerto Rican girl, tries to come to terms with her painful past as she waits to
see if her uncle recovers from injuries he suffered when the towers collapsed on September 11, 2001.
  ISBN 978-0-06-244759-3

  1. September 11 Terrorist Attacks, 2001—Juvenile fiction.   [1. September 11 Terrorist Attacks,
2001—Fiction.   2. Uncles—Fiction.   3. New York (N.Y.)—Fiction.   4. Puerto Ricans—Fiction.]
I. Title.
PZ7.H432135Ci 2005   2004026185
[Fic]—dc22

Typography by Alicia Mikles
16 17 18 19 20   PC/RRDH   10 9 8 7 6 5 4 3 2 1
❖
Revised paperback edition, 2016

For my lovely cousin,
Nanú Paloma Quintana Guerrero,
February 2, 1978–August 4, 2003, in memory

For all the Cinnamon Girls

See the steel of Tompkins gate bent back and wise
See the dead grass that fights to climb and rise
See that boy trippin' into a cool pool of dirty moonlight
See that girl lickin' her pocked arm as if sugar bright
See the last limbs of autumn, frayed and yet, still alive
See those kids lean on the fence as if their secret knife
See the wind scoot and scoop their last ragged sighs
See the leaves drift away and tremble by the cellar ice
See that muchacha swaying to a song in the fiery storm
See my shadow dancing to its own silence—so alone.

Canelita, lower east side, nyc

Cinnamon Girl

9/19/01 Wednesday night, Lower East Side, hospital,
4th floor

wrapped in gauze

Uncle DJ's
wrapped in gauze.

He dreams inside a foreign *islita*
that no one has discovered except himself.
There are congas under a tropical moon
gold nectar saxophones and pale blue-blue maraca stars.
The galaxy spins and then fire-bursts into a bird
from San Juan,

wings red-red as the Flamboyan tree,
and it speaks with the dark cinnamon of
the Caribbean night. Its eyes are aquamarine and
when it sings green-green rain pours and the soft
island sways to a hip-hop mambo of *amor*, then
adios. But—

I don't want to say adios.

Tape across the mouth
hands strapped
to the side of the hospital bed rails.

IV and blood bottle lines tangle
down to uncle DJ's arm.
A Darth Vader machine beeps
every time he breathes through a sky-white
see-through hose down his throat.

Sweep my thin hand across the bed rail
just in case there is dust
gnawing around the chrome.

Uncle DJ's swallowed enough dust—
two buildings of dust, Twin Towers of dust.
Last week, he called mamá Mercedes and said,
Hey sis, gotta do something—I came to deliver roses,
as usual, ya' know. A jet or something hit Tower One.
A blast, and then, another. Now, I gotta do something.
There's fire and screams all around.

Eleven thirty pm.
News TV. Blue flash inside

the eerie hospital room. Tía Gladys
talks loud to Mamá:
What's happening to my city?
The feeling's gone, Mercedes. The *melao'* is missin'.
Yolanda María is my *melao'*, Mamá says.

Last night I dreamt
I went with Mamá and tía Gladys to Ground Zero.

Tía Gladys digs
with her glossy orange fingernails.
A police dog barks and digs-digs too.
There is a tiny cone,
a hole
full of black nothing and tapping—
deep below the rubble. A moan. A long moan
from underground. Echoes up Canal Street to Chambers.
Rubble echoes—one hundred feet high of broken
steel bones and tiny lives crushed forever.

Echo. Echo.
Sálvamelo, tía Gladys prays out loud
in her plastic tiger-print jacket,
Diosito sálvamelo, save him for me,

Haré lo que quieras, I'll do whatevah.
She makes a *manda*, a promise
like she did when mamá Mercedes told her
last month that I was getting into trouble
at Longfellow School in West Liberty, Iowa.

She promised *La Virgencita*
that she would take us in
so I could get better. This morning,

tía Gladys mumbles another manda, something
about going back to Puerto Rico and helping
poor kids in Aguas Buenas.

In my dream,
*Mamá and aunt Gladys
kneel down slow on the sharp dust of the World
Trade Center—like a church all broken.
A rescue worker with a dog says
I can hear him tapping . . .
tap, tap, tap!
Rescue Company #1
on his bitten shirt.*

All of a sudden, bam! Like the crushed
tower, my throat gets fiery, then empty
in the hospital room—uncle DJ!
I want to shout louder than
the Darth Vader machine. *Nada, Nada.*
Say something! Rezzy, my cool friend
from PS 1486, elbows me and says
in her typical English accent, Wula,
say something, Yolanda!

Rezzy's from Kuwait, new here too,
like me, tenth grade. Rezzy's hazel eyes
glow by the candlelight.
Are those the secret things that you
promised you would show me?

It's jes' a cereal box,
with my writing and some letters inside.
Pull them out in little bundles tied together with
red strings. Untie one and read it.
Maybe uncle DJ will hear me and wake up, I tell Rezzy.
Maybe, she says. Jes' maybe.

෴

June 10, 01

Dear Canelita,

My sister said your papi Reinaldo got you
a weasel or something. So that you could feel better,
you know, about Sky gone. So what you gonna do?
Flirt with *la weasel* instead of talking to me?

Love con windy skies,
Uncle DJ

P.S. Write me.

May 5, 01

Querida Carnelita,

Been visiting tía Aurelia in San Francisco
for a few weeks.
Hope she gets better soon. Or I'll lose my job at
Rosie's Roses back in Nueva York.

San Francisco on a Saturday's just like Puerto Rico.
Well, you know what I mean, *nena—la playa, la música*.
Man, haven't been here for so looong! Born here
right after the Army transferred my pops from Puerto Rico to
Treasure Island. Boom! He met my mamá Angeles at the
Golden Gate Theatre off of Market Street.
¡Oye, fíjate! Just like that!
Watching Al Capone with Rod Steiger and Faye Dunaway
con popcorn. From *coquitos to coctails de camarón*.
Back in '57.
After that stint, we moved to the nearest salsa center in
the City, right where your tía Aurelia lives now,
in the Mission District where
Pops did odd jobs to make ends meet
until he passed away in '78.
That's about the same time Gladys's papi went AWOL
in New Jersey and ran to the border because
he didn't like the food.
Guess where the border was? *Loisaida*!
Or as you say, Alphabet City.
You can't beat that with a pair of *timbales*!
Guess what?
Just today, while I was buying tortillas at La Palma,
I got a little taste of Willie Colón. Man, he was hitting

the trombone like I hit Abuelita's *gandinga*. He was busting up
the streets. I love this city. Thinking of my Canelita.

Amor con chocolate,
Uncle DJ

P.S. How's school in West Liver? Happy *Cinco de Mayo*!

∽

Yo', your uncle DJ was so cool,
Rezzy whispers as I drop the letters
back into the cereal box in my backpack.

A fine-tuned voice from the Twin Towers
sings from afar—*I wanted to help. So,
I stayed holding her hands.*

The voice
sounds like a violin.

Each word is a note
each note is a heart.

Papi says,
Every heart
sings forever.

Roses so light
in feathery sight
high above
bitter clouds
broken stems and infinite particles
their hands
wrapped
as
they rise
and

F

     A

     L

     L

to me. Come then, come
so I can water you, give you
my breath.

Squeeze Rezzy's hand. A few days ago
a rush of letters
lifted uncle DJ onto a stretcher
covered in dirt, half blue, almost gone,
a cocoon caked in gray-white.
His tongue made of chalk—I wrote
the letters on my hand,

FBI
DEA

ATF
FDNY

Why do you write? Why
do you keep these old letters?
Rezzy asks me. I say nothing.

Write to hold back my tears. Write
with my hard eyes open wide in the hospital room
flickering with candles, yellow, green,
red-red.

sky

Yo' Moondragon!

Marietta snags me by the stairs
on the way to class. *Mondragón*, I say in a whisper.
Moondragooon! Marietta smacks me on the back,
like she does every time she sees me.
Floats away cool with her little gang—
Fat RGB with crazy colored hair
and his boney boy, Lil' Weez. And, of course
there's Shannon Iler who's always laughing
and Zako, Marietta's pimple-necked boyfriend.

Marietta turns back,
struts up to me, shouts out,
Moondragon, with your brain-a-saggin',
say something, freak!
Pulls my cheeks like Silly Putty.

She lets go, and cracks up, walks off,
her jeans so tight her hair stubble pops out.
Zako, with thick eyebrows and a sneaky smile

pulls her to him and turns to me, smirks
with his teeth out. Rezzy jumps in
and hauls me away.
You forget them,
she says and asks me if I am going to visit
Uncle DJ at the hospital tonight. Bite my lips,
stare down hard as we walk silent down the hall.
Scrape my fingernails against the walls of cartoons
and crooked lockers all the way to Mrs. Lucy Camacho's
English class. Think of Longfellow school,
my school in Iowa. Think of my friend, Sky,

laying
down on the highway looking up at the stars,
playing "Chicken" with Cheyenne, a runaway boy
that I liked kinda. Wonder what she was looking at
so far away. Is uncle DJ looking up there too?
Gotta take care of him. Like he took care of me
and even ol' mean tía Aurelia in San Francisco.

∾

May 9, 01

Dear Canelita mía,

Don't worry when you read this. Ok?
Took tía Aurelia to St. Luke's hospital again where we
had to wait for hours until they checked her into the
fluoroscope room. Man, was she jumping mad at me
afterwards. As a matter of fact she's still not talking to me.
They made her drink a gallon of gray malt so that they
could trace it in her *tripas*. The doctors think she has a
hernia in her esophagus. *Es la pobreza*, she tells me.
All those years of wishing I could eat all the food *los ricos*
had on the table while I scrubbed their floors on my knees.
I got blisters on my lips from looking at the T-bone steaks!
Then she laughs.
She always tells me the same story about working
in Miami in the thirties, about how she worked as a maid
in the resorts and as a salad girl at the Plaza Hotel
in Manhattan in the late forties. Makes me sad, Canelita.
That's why I want you to go to school too and not be
like me taking odd jobs, playing congas in small-time
bands, being a part-time DJ, or delivering cakes, pizzas
and even flowers for Valentine's Day.

That's the only real gig I got . . . delivering flowers for
Rosie's Roses for All Occasions back home in Loisaida.
Promise me you'll be the first one to make it
all the way to *colegio*.

Love con mangos,
Uncle DJ

P.S. Oh, I forgot to tell you that I borrowed a pair of
Latin Percussions from Babatunde. Man, I was hotter
than *sofrito*, I was *el rey del cuero*, well, almost.
Abraham, one of the guys here from Ghana was on fire.
And guess what? I dedicated a song to you.

◎◎

cinnamon girl

Mamá Mercedes pins up photos
of Aguas Buenas on the wall.
No hay mal que por bien venga,
There's always some good with the bad.
She's always making up words like that
you'd think she was born to be a gypsy
or an opera singer.

Tía Gladys unmakes
and makes a funky altar like Mamá in Iowa—
A San Martín de Caballero statue and another
of La Virgen María with roses by the window,
a basket of mangoes, candles, candles, candles,
velas, velas, velas and a heavy boom box.
There's always room for a rumba or merengue,
Chica, they'll nevah know if this is a hospital room
or a salsa club, she tells me with a half smile.
Tía kneels by uncle DJ's bed.
Mamá sits quietly next to her.
Beto can hear the music, Chica, tía Gladys

says as she pats uncle DJ on the forehead
with a towelette. Ya' know, that's how I met him.

I'd go to "Rap Nites" at Negril's on 2nd and 11th Street,
there he was in the crowd, with *los jevos*, DJ Kool Herc
and FabFiveFreddy.
Tía Gladys wants to tell me a happy story and
then she stops and drops her head on Mamá's lap.
Say something, Yolanda, she whimpers.

Está bién, todo está bién,
Mamá says in a thick voice. Brushes Tía's long
blackish hair with her fingers.
Yolanda's like me, remember? Never said a thing,
bendito, 'til I was twenty-nine.
Mamá lowers her head and speaks soft words.
Never was allowed to go out with a man
until my thirties. I wanted to be a dancer,
remember, Gladys?

Well, with that stubborn half brother Tito of yours,
contrayao', I bet you couldn't even put on new shoes,
especially red ones!

Tía Gladys half jokes from the floor,
plays with a handkerchief.

I pull out a couple more letters
so I can pretend uncle DJ is talking to me.

๛

Dear Canela,

Just a few blocks from where I am standing,
the old Fantasy Records building glows in the sun.
That's where Mongo Santamaría, Paul Desmond
and Cal Tjader put their música together. Maybe
this summer I'll drive from Loisaida and pick
you up and I'll show you the place. Just wait, when I
get back to New York I am gonna build me a recording
studio like no other, on the roof, *el rufeh*, it's gonna
be just like the old days, I'll be mixin' and blastin'
música like I used to at the Rockland Parkway, I am gonna
build it on top of the world, well, on top of Loisaida, and

maybe you can help me, we'll call it *RadioSabor*! And
we'll paint it like the Fanstasy Records building, all dressed
up in candy colors, with murals, you gotta come here,
check it out for yourself so you can see what I am saying . . .
right? Your tía Aurelia would love to see you too.
We're gonna stay with her for a while, well, on the floor.
La viejita is still strong
but I am afraid she may go any day too. Pray
to San Martín de Caballero, bendito, you know what I mean.
Keeping an eye on her making sure her *esófago'* heals.
Not to mention her anemia and her heart!
She's a walking Puerto Rican Revolution.

Love con *arroz y lechón*,
Uncle DJ

P.S. Your tía Gladys can't wait to call you tonight.
She says you better be off the phone too.

ͼͽ

Siéntate,
Come sit down, Mamá tells tía Gladys.
They both grow small and quiet in the cold

room beeping with a little television
by uncle DJ's head. It makes wavy lines,

comets
in electric dust and shooting stars
in yellow frosty light.

I move up to him, his eyes closed
and whisper into his ear—

Uncle DJ,
This is Yolanda, your cinnamon girl.
Remember you called me Canelita,
how you sent me letters in Iowa,
when I was feeling so lost, after my friend
Sky died and you told me how music fills
the holes in your heart and how you wanted
me to help you build RadioSabor on your rufeh,
a little music station on the roof where I could help you
mix sounds like you used to at Rockland Parkway
and listen to your Willie Colón albums, you
promised to tell me all the family secretos like when
tía Gladys's father, Fernando, went AWOL
in New Jersey because he didn't like the mashed potatoes

in the navy . . . I won't tell, just like your letters,
I keep them all sealed in a cereal box, well,
anyway, just want to tell you
that I am going to make a manda too, a promise
for you. My manda is, uh,

I am going to build RadioSabor
on the rufeh-roof, and let all your music out
for the Lower East Side to hear, I mean, Loisaida,
like you always say, all the world
will hear your music, uncle DJ,
but I won't say nada to nobody right now
this is just between you—and me.

Just then uncle DJ's eyes open,
well, barely.
And I hear a voice in my head:

Help the others, Canelita . . .
You must save the others . . .
the others . . .

Who, uncle DJ?
Rock back with Mamá and tía Gladys, asleep.
The others—

where are they now?
How will I
find them?

witchy wind

A witchy wind
swells above the gray city.

On a dirty bus,
for a ride, going nowhere
in the fuzzy smog, metal seats. Tía Gladys
and Mamá. Rezzy with me
on the front seat. Cicatríz, my pet ferret,
snuggles on my shoulder. Papi found her in a train,
told me, Just don't give her human food.
We pass a firehouse on West 10th.

Rezzy laughs out loud when
I tell her about how Papi feeds Cicatríz in a shoe.
Rezzy's got raggedy green bell-bottoms
and my plastic panther-black jacket,
her hair in spirals
under a funky Yankees cap.

Where are they—*los firefighters*?
Mamá asks no one.

Where are the others?
I ask myself. The others . . .

The firehouse looks tired,
ancient, beaten. Nearby,
at St. Vincent's Hospital,
there are hundreds of people crowding
to read little posters with photographs.
They read and hold each other
at the same time.
On what floor?
Someone asks out loud. Maybe she stopped
for breakfast and wasn't there.

Hundreth floor, Yola! A little dusty voice
crawls up my sleeve and tucks itself into my ear.

Another voice says—
I stayed, no way out, dear, just fire.

It's ok, Yolanda
Mother was waiting for me.

I grasp at the air
as if whisking away a strange butterfly.

Whatya doing, wula, are you falling asleep?
Rezzy asks. Says wula for everything.

Remember when you first came to school?
All you did was sit in the back of Mrs. Camacho's class
and scribble-scribble. Rezzy kicks my backpack.
Who were you writing to?
I don't know, I tell Rezzy.
After the towers went down,
so many words came rushing out of me
more than ever before.

Open my backpack
and show Rezzy—

ෙ

d us t voi ces

Near the Exodus Boxing Gym.
Peek out from my classroom window.
Just printed the date on my poetry assignment,
September 20th.

Gaze
freeze. The rose
grows. Tiny
petals
flare
again, dust
voices. Some
open toward   me.
others mix
into the empty
sky. A new   sky

covers me. And i cover it
with my sky.

September 20, 01

**a thousand little days i
keep secret**

Today
lasts
forever.

School
trembles. Blocks crumble—
next block, Avenue C
C for crumbleagain.
Sister Lopez's Tarot Card Shoppe,
school floats in
between

no night. Stay
awake, Yolanda stay
awake in a
thousand little days i
keep   secret
inside my head.

September 21, 01

o positive

Helicopters chopchop
spray find
dive deep
hoses stretch hiss

bulldozers cranes cameras flash
dump trucks line up
for 20 blocks
aid workers wrap the street
Cup-a-Soup 123
baskets of cheeseburgers
Chelsea Piers turns
into an emergency room
Hudson River and 23rd Street
Rabbis and fries
EMTs and med students
O positive
bloodlines—

O positive?
Thass me.

September 22, today

∞

Back on the street, Loisaida.
Rezzy flies home
on her scratched-up skateboard.

I wear
purple everything. Or black.
Tops
and pants, sneakers too. I go slow.
A so-what
slow. But fast on the way to Shorty's *bodega*
by Tompkins Square Park and East 8th.
Grab a cola, lean cool on the iron gates.
Notice the whirls of
fine-sharp cloud dust mix
into the dark hairs
on my arms.

9/23/01 Sunday, Sister Lopez's Tarot Card Shoppe, Loisaida,
afternoon
strong, 'juerte

After Tía's *gandules*,
I race to my room. Sofa room

with a glassy bead curtain separating it
from the living room,
Cicatríz on my shoulder. Uncle DJ calls it
the Everything Room because it's a place of mambos
and *fútbol*, corner kitchen of home cooking like
tostones and *pasteles*, everybody always talking, singing.
Hot orange posters of Puerto Rican boxers on the wall—
Wilfredo Benitez, Carlos Ortiz and Tía's favorite,
Felix Trinidad, and little photos of grandfather
Salomé carrying his black *machete* in Cidra.
Papi Reinaldo and Mamá on one corner,
tía Gladys on the other. I push through the glassy red beads,
listen to sirens outside and grab my backpack
with raisin cookies for Cicatríz.

Sometimes, after
everyone is asleep tía Gladys snores.

Spotlight my flashlight
on her honey-colored belly, heh-heh.

I go to
the brown dry bathroom. In front of the mirror—
over the homemade *tendedero,* wiggle
my red plumpy tongue.
Wiggle in the

D
    A
    R
    K

        L
        I
           G
           H

                T

I remember
liking myself.

My own few, wild, funny
faces.

The Everything Room is waxy and still as the saints
on Mamá's altar. You can hear each bead knock-knock
on my fingernails like a rosary. Chipped paint
by the light switch cracks and I rush out
to meet Rezzy, we run through Avenue C. Run-run past

wet black cellars, Shorty's Liquors,
the trashjunk gardens,
stop, rub my eyes,
didn't sleep much last night.

We go quiet
to Sister Lopez's Tarot Card Shoppe
to hang out, buy roses for uncle DJ's room.
Mamá works here part-time,
I tell Rezzy. She should be here
any minute. There's confections, gypsy clothes,
incense and cool gold string rings too.
Rezzy, Rezzy,
poke her in the ribs, You gotta help me
find the others. Okeh? Okeh?

Still can see Rezzy
the first day I met her, just a couple
of months ago. She looked like a little round lawyer.
Briefcase, blue shirt, black tie and a light blue pinafore.
What's a pinafore? Something
you wear while you play piano?
I asked her. Almost look the same. Same hair, same eyes,
same-same except she's big and I am so-sooo skinny.

Now she tries on a plastic zebra-striped jacket
from Sister Lopez's clearance rack.

Floppy shark-tooth lapels,
like the one uncle DJ sent me last summer.

How do you like my new style from "da village,"
Rezzy says making a funny face and wobbling her head.
She slumps her shoulders and
sits next to a rough-faced black cat.
Ummie and Papa
want me to just be me, but uncle Rummi
who I stay with says
In America, be American!

Like you, Yo'!

We sit on the floor by the velvet handbags
with Egyptian pyramids and girls' faces,
one eye outlined in charcoal mascara.

Read me some more of your letters, Yo',
Rezzy peeks into my backpack. Your letters,
wula!

ஒ

March 2, 01

Dear uncle DJ,

Say gracias
to tía Gladys for sending me the two CDs
and a book of poems by Julia de Burgos.
But I don't understand them, weird. Anyway,
I am so excited. I'll be thirteen next month
and guess what? If we move, I'll be going
to City High next year, in Iowa City.
Papi was right, there's a lot of Mexicanos here.
But they don't speak. Well, English. Dunno,
Hello? Told Papi that I think we are the only
Puerto Ricans in the whole state of Iowa.

Maraca! He shouted and laughed.
Am I a maraca, uncle DJ?

Love con toasted baseball game peanuts,
Canela

P.S. Ma ra ca, ha!

March 7, 01

Dear Canelita,

Corazonsito,
You are not a maraca,
You are a lovely *manguito* or should I say *manguita*?
How about a *guayabita*? Sounds funny, huh?
Gonna borrow a pair of congas from Babatunde,
one of the best congeros in The City. See ya'.

Amor con *pescao' frito,*
uncle DJ

P.S. Hip-Hop? I'll let you in on a *secreto.*
I was right there in the middle of it when it started.

March 14, 01

Dear Canela,

Didn't get a chance to talk to you last night
about my early DJ days like I promised you.
Let me tell you,
I started my DJ *cosa* back in the early eighties,
when Hip-Hop was just comin' on with the NYC Breakers,
that's when Rock Steady was the *mero-mero* and the Roxy
was the only Hip-Hop club in Manhattan.
Shudda seen your tía! *Cheverisima!*
Well, gotta go and hustle gigs, jobs
and pay *los biles*—and take care of your tía Aurelia.
Still dreamin' of those sweet days in Noba' Yor.

Your tío DJ

P.S. Got a feeling my job at Rosie's Roses is gone.
Don't matter, she'll make room for me. I am her best
delivery man.

∾

Look, Rezzy
You gotta help me find the others, I whisper
and take her behind the crystal balls and incense burners,
Rezzy, please, so uncle DJ will live,
I made a manda.
What are you talking about? She says.
Maybe I can help you,
an old woman with a husky voice croons.
She has a thin long nose, thick
ruby lips and green glasses,
her hair is night-black pulled back into a braid.
With wine-red ribbons, coarse turquoise silk shirt
half open with an old gold *virgensita*, hanging
from her neck.

Sister Lopez sits down
opens her large hands
and raises them as if feeling the heat
of the table puffing up from an oven below the floor.

I am Sister Lopez, been here since
the days when we took over Tompkins Park, snatched
it back from the city peoples
like a spider steals a fly, niña.

Sister Lopez peers into me,
kinda dreamy and then looks at Rezzy. Sister Lopez
pulls out a deck of cards from her breast pocket
and leans over the round glass table between us.
Asks me to shuffle the deck, worn with little moons
in persimmon colors, soft as feathers. A card printed
with nine floating gold coins flips out by itself.
Someone
is calling you, niña, she says before I finish.
The calling is strong, *juerte*.

*9/24/01 Monday, PS 1486, Mrs. Lucy Camacho's
English class*
white stairs

Mrs. Camacho slides back her wire rims
over her oily nose and scribbles a poem
by Joey Piñero on the board.
Something about the barrio and whoknowswhat,
then she asks us to read it aloud. Everything has changed,
she says, Things aren't all *chulisnaquis*, so cool, ya' know?
You gotta do something, are you listenin'?
Take out your letters to the president, she asks us,
and then sits in front of the class, picks an
autumn leaf from her hair. Half of it
dipped in fire, the other half in
lemony moonlight.

Marietta squirts a little box of Hawaiian Punch
into her mouth
and slams her head down on her desk. Alma and
Carmela, the twins, pass tiny notes next to me.

Jenikajade and McKenzie
whisper something to Rezzy,

something about Marietta and Zako
getting high last week and standing
on a roller coaster.

Thinking of Sister Lopez and what she told me—
"Strong, 'juerte," a voice calling. And
what she said after that.

School here so easy, Yo', Rezzy jabbers behind me
while she plays with my hair. Back home, right now
I'd have to take the CBSE, wula!
The what?
The Central Board Secondary Education Exam!
Rezan Sabah! Maybe you two want to visit
Principal Giannoni this morning?
Mrs. Camacho says almost politely
by the overhead projector showing
Marietta's letter that starts with curly
loopy letters. Mrs. Camacho turns off the light
so we can read it out loud:

Dear Mr. President,

Big letters. Big deal.

I turn away and put my ear to my desk.
Sister Lopez's husky voice comes to me.

Down the long white stairs in the night
All the falling voices you will cure of fright
You cannot show your face
You cannot leave a trace
Do this with all your heart and all your might
And your uncle will rest in the highest place.

Sister Lopez's low voice circles me. Nah,
it's nothing, just spooky-smokey words,
like her cheap incense.
Rezzy says in class, half dark. Sometimes
uncle Rummi sounds spooky too when he talks
of Kuwait and the Royals
driving in their Rolls-Royces around the block
spitting nondigestible chocolate until they go crazy.
Or when he talks of the Gulf War and how he
couldn't find his gas mask in the kitchen, wula!

Later, we leap
across the curb outside school and run by my building

up, up, floor after floor until we are out of breath
on the rufeh. The sky wrinkled and droopy with ash.

This is where
you will help me collect voices, Rezzy.
This is where you will help me build RadioSabor.
Ah. *Ahh.*

9/25/01 Tuesday, on the rufeh, Loisaida tenements,
evening
RadioSabor

On the rufeh,

guzzling sodas and chomping lime-flavored
Cheetos we got from Shorty's bodega.
Saw Zako, from class, with cork skin,
he leaned so cool on the iron gates at the park and
so skinny-skinny sucking a tobacco-smeared pipe,
staring through the swings going back and forth, going.
Wonder what he was seeing? Wonder.

Now tell me, Yo', what radio thing are you
talking about?
Hold on, I say, picking some poems
from my cereal box, then I lean over
the edge of the rufeh and sniff the air, sniff,
sniff. Smells like alcohol,
burnt perfume, eggs and a bloody nose. Blood
always reminds me of Christmas because dead flowers
smell like dried blood. But it's not Christmas.

I hear sirens, maybe like the ones
that cried when the rescue workers
dug uncle DJ out of the earth.
Like the ones in my dream . . .
men in yellow raincoats
and orange striped vests,
steel hats, buckets
of ashes, wires and dirt, FDNY and NYPD
on their shirts—
bulldozers and dump trucks
and sirens fading in and
out.
Sniff, sniff,
read softly.

∽

sofrito

On the miniature stove,
tía Gladys stirs sofrito
on a pebbly black caldero—
our makeshift kitchen
in the Everything Room.
Mamá washes more cilantro,

a bouquet she can afford.
Then, garlic, onions and green peppers.
Look at her so tiny, still
with watery
dark eyes and her heart
bigger than the chopping block,
her sofrito art
for me.

August 16, 01

nod, nod

Morning black *cafecito*
mamá Mercedes sips slow, stares out
our tenement window to *quiensabedonde*—I close
my eyes.
PS 1486.
New school since we arrived this summer.
Ninth. A crate of windows made of chalk,
huddled boys and girls that stare cold.
I doze off.
Say,

Mamá talks to me serious
in a thread thin voice,
Dime algo, Yolanda María. Please
say—something. *No seas
abochorrna' como yo,* Don't be
so embarrassed like I was.
Nod,   nod
then I smile
sunflowers in one
second.

September 5, 01

rumblesdown

i   want
to be a dust flower
a light
gray
rose.

words in my head.
i want to speak them—then they c
rumble

float to the ground. Lift them up
that's all i can do now,
come on, lift
them just like
this.

September 14, 01

☙

There goes your tía Gladys!
Rezzy grabs the poems from my hand
and points down the street.

Yeah, she's going
to Seven Happiness Café by Houston Street
where she works as a *mesera*, a waitress, on Tuesdays
through Fridays. Every time I pass by
I wave. On the weekends she colors hair
at Tunomás Honey Hair Salon.

And my mamá cooks and cleans at home,
or you can find her sweeping the incense
dust at Sister Lopez's place.
Mamá's always telling me, Life ain't peachy,

La vida no es un güame. I wish she'd speak in English,
it's embarrass . . .

Yolandah, Yolandah!
A voice
pops out
from my purple-gray paw-print top,
up windy by my belly button.
Hurry up!

Get those flowerpots, I yell to Rezzy
and that pile of dirty wood panels.
Okeh, okeh, we are workin' on it, okeh,
rumble downstairs and grab Papi's hammers
and a baby bag of nails.
Okeh, okeh, and pick up whatever chipped pieces
of broken plates and more wet wood. Okeh, okeh
and one of uncle DJ's handpainted signs
that reads **RadioSabor** and there it is!

Uh-oh,
I forgot the plastic garbage bags for windows
and the door, thass right. Now step inside,
huddle under the hard crooked tent and

sit down on milk crates. Hold Rezzy's hand.
Tight. Tight.

This is our station, Rezzy. On top of the world.
This is where we will play uncle DJ's music
so he will live, I whisper,
lean my head on Rezzy's head, until

we're almost one body
that barely breathes
in little teary hiccups,
so, so
he, he,
will live.

9/26/01 Wednesday, RadioSabor, after school, Loisaida rufeh
cereal box

Are
the voices coming
Yo'? Yo'?

Rezzy asks me inside our RadioSabor tent.
Just play this, I tell her.
We slip off our headphones, hang them
on the wire antennas and bump up the volume.
Play J. Lo and Arsenio
from uncle DJ's collection.
I would've brought my boom boxer, Yo',
but uncle Rummi thinks I am at the library.
Boom box! I tell her, Not boom boxer!

Turn up the volume all the way.
Pick at a tiny plate of Mamá's sofrito,
and set it on a milk crate. Fried garlic, onions,
cilantro makes the spirits happy, I make up a story
and explain it to Rezzy. She ignores me.
Lights a blue candle and a stick of sandalwood.

It's like playing house but
with a little altar. Eh?
Yeah, yeah, I say.

The aromas mix
and make me dreamy. Remember

when we got here a few months ago,
after two years of living in Iowa. Papi's idea.
You gotta move, nena, if you stand still you turn
into stone. Move-move, breathe under the sky,
make your own islita wherevah you go.
So, we went to West Liberty, Iowa, 'cause that's
where my papi's cucumber-shaped pickup
broke down, was supposed to make it to San Francisco
so we could hook up with my oldest tía, my tía Aurelia
and maybe Papi could get a job at the Fairmont Hotel
where you can see famous people like James Brown. But,
tía Aurelia is too mean and just talks about going back
to San Juan, and makes me say all kinds of prayers
every hour like you swear the world is ending all the time.

So Papi
worked for the Muscatine Sausage & Poultry Company,

taking care of millions of chickens
in four long stanky houses
and he'd bring some home, swing them in the air,
by their crazy heads, their feet
whirling like busted jump ropes.
And he slammed them
against the fence.
That's how the Mexicanos do it, he would say.
We living a new life now, nena, he said,
just like I promised.

Promises, promises.
Open my backpack and stare inside.
Got more letters, Yo'? Read me one of yours,
Yo'? Please?

∞

April 8, 01

Dear uncle DJ,

Got your postcard of the Golden Gate. Showed it to my
teacher at Longfellow.

He liked what you said when you wrote,
"The Golden Gate is like a funky Brooklyn Bridge dipped
in hot sauce and love."
It takes a lot for my teacher, Mr. Rolodex, to smile,
well, that's not his name-name.
Me and my friend Sky call him that because his desk is
always a mess and he needs to get himself organized.
He couldn't figure out my poetry,
said it was about seeing things
before they happen, yeah, right.
Have you ever seen Iowa rain?
It's thick as nails. And I am not that skinny anymore.
Yesterday, I pulled Mamá out on the porch
(they have those here)
and made her dance with me—in the rain!
We were so chévere, so cool!
Did I tell you that I have lots of boy friends?
Let me tell you,
Rudy Fink, Matt Drury, Jason Estrada, Adolfo Robles,
Sammy Ketchenblauer or something like that
and Reymundo Arreglado, he's so cute.
I am also good at sports, did I tell you?
Soccer, kickball, dodgeball, basketball, skating, running,
swimming, baseball, football and Ping-Pong!

I think I am the first porto'rican that knows how to play
Ping-Pong!
You'd love our new house, well, it's an old one but I have
a room all to myself
and a mirror—and a bed.

Write me sooner,
Love, your Canelita,

Y

ை

Tell me about Sammy Ketchupflour, Rezzy asks.
And Sky. Did she ever stay over? Is she tall?

Yolanda María! Mamá calls.
Where are you? Come down here right now!

We have to go to the hospital, Dr. Weisberg says.
It's time.

Time?
Time?

9/27/01 Thursday, intensive care unit, evening
absolutely nothing but night

Roberto had two seizures, Mrs. Santos.
We are going to take him in for a scan.
Dr. Weisberg says to tía Gladys
in a soft voice. I really thought it was his time.
We wait, wait
for the orderly to come and
get him ready.

Uncle DJ's chest goes up, down, the oxygen
in, out, in ocean sounds, wind and skies
mixing inside his body, he is light, nothing.
Tictic, I hear
a clock snap, little gears buzz and
make his finger jitter, deep water swishes
and bubbles in a broken fountain inside his throat,
no voice—

Bend
into his ear again,

Uncle DJ, uncle DJ,
it's Cinnamon Girl.

I made a manda for you,
played J. Lo and Arsenio,
your favorites, well, J. Lo
is my favorite, on the rufeh.

Put my headphones
on his pillow and play the wavy beats.
Can you hear that, uncle DJ? Thass it.

When you take out the tubes?
Tía Gladys asks Dr. Weisberg,
patting down one of the plastic packs
on the IV rack with the orderly.

Dr. Weisberg's eyes soften.
Something's keeping him going. I guess,
as soon as he can breathe on his own.
He says kinda quiet. Dr. Weisberg
checks uncle DJ's pulse.
He's got a strong heart, Mrs. Santos.

Leaves with uncle DJ.
The door opens and closes,
Breathes in, then out. In and out
they are the same.

Light
dust
tumbles down to my
shredded shoe
laces.

'Juerte, 'juerte, Beto. Be strong.
Tía Gladys says
and leans into the menthol breeze
of the shiny nurses' station.

Open my backpack
grab my cereal box and pull out a poem.

෨

bluish habichuelas

*Night's when i listen to uncle DJ's songs
from his tenement rooftop—RadioSabor*

Porto'rican Oldies, he would say.
Machito and 'ol time güagüancó's with Celia Cruz
while tía Gladys swings her hips under
our ceiling, dreamy under
the chalky sky dots
bluish habichuelas of the Milky Way.

Así, así
like this, Yola! Tía Gladys kinda smiles.
Night
Where are you?

September 24, 01

ins ide

Put
one
hand
over my
eyes.
Then, the other hand. Petal
hands.
Drag my feet

to school. Peek
through
my fingers.

Dust inside
the dust. i want to
laugh at my serious face
in the girl's bathroom.

September 24, 01

∞

Mamá and I sit alone. Clean the dust
on uncle DJ's bed rail. Wait. Wait.

Rub my neck, Yolanda, por favor.
Mamá's always hurting. Always aching.
Her skin is smooth and young, a yellow-brown
from not enough sunlight maybe,
and her hair is long and dry. Rub her neck.
Face the empty bed, twisted and tired.

Mandas don't work,
they just make things worse! I grumble
and scratch Mamá's neck by accident.

Mamá turns and pinches my arm.
The virgencita on a thin gold chain
around her neck swings out and lands
outside her collar.

I am not leaving here, Yolanda María!
That's my manda, okeh, Mamá says in
her stubborn scratchy voice.
She lets go of my arm, smoothes
the red blotchy pinch-star on my skin.
Her virgencita slips back into her blouse.

Feel like running. Run
into the avenues,
let them run through me too, run, run
full of absolutely nothing but
night.

9/28/01 Friday, tenement kitchen, Loisaida, early morning
rooster claw

Just Papi and me.
On opposite sides of the Everything Room.
Mamá and Tía are at the hospital.

Play with a thimble
from Mamá's Puerto Rico
of *colmados* where she listens to tía Aurelia's stories or
visits Don Arturo's shop where he teaches her
how to roll cigars. She's twelve, has a birthday *trulla*
and strolls to the playas and
tosses a seashell into the waters
mirroring back to the
sandy sparkles in her hair.

Maybe in that green-blue water there is
a silvery thread of my hair. Play, play.

What did Sister Lopez mean?
Squeeze out my cereal box
and squint at my poetry sheets.

Down the long white stairs in the night
All the falling voices you will cure of fright
You cannot show your face
You cannot leave a trace
Do this with all your heart and all your might
And your uncle will rest in the highest place.

What stairs?
White? Falling?

Fold the inky sheets and slide them back
slow into the cereal box . . . shhh
push it slowly under my sofa so Papi
won't wake up.

He tosses in his sofa corner.
Snores. Mumbles.

In Iowa he used to come home all drowsy
with beer and sing out,
Yola, did you know
that you can make seventy-nine
by-products with chicken?

Fridays he would stumble home
swaying from side to side and say,
A rooster claw can be sanded into gambling dice.
That's why the devil has rooster feet!

On my last birthday, he fell and bounced
on the bed facedown with his chicken-parts apron
and his rubber chicken bloody boots
and mumbled, Did I tell you I invented
Chickabree?
That was supposed to be
some kinda tortilla-shaped chicken chip
that flies like a Frisbee. Not funny. That's when
he saw me crying and made his manda.

From now on,
he said pulling me hard by the arm
from the living room all the way to the porch,
No more *trago*, no more drink, eh, chica?
and, your papi's gonna study, one
of these days, maybe, be a lawyer.
One day . . . and you will be proud, eh?
Papi threw his arms wild around me
to kiss me, saying and spitting,

Perdóname, I am sorrrry, Yolandita,
slipping off the porch down the stairs
to the street. You're always saying that,
I wanted to scream but I didn't, just
ran out into the night, my head down
seeing my feet slap the dark road, hitch rides
to the 620 Club where Cheyenne and Sky
hung out.

Papi tosses on the sofa, wakes up
blinks at me for a second, rubs his eyes.
Buttons his shirt, one of uncle DJ's shirts
with palm-tree islands and flying saxophones on it.
Goes back to sleep with one arm
slung over his face. Papi's always tossing
and turning. Alone. With red eyes,
smoking his cigarros. Handsome and alone.
Wish I knew what's inside his head. Why
he stares at me and says nothing and
then all of a sudden

he gives me a fake ruby ring. Or he buys me
dictionaries from used book tables on the street
and leaves them on my bed.

Mamá says I am like him, 'cause she never
knows what I am doing next, look like him too,
dark brown, a brown-red, fiery.

A hot airy wind comes to me. Papi's island shirt
gives me an idea. Pack some clothes fast.

Stuff sloppy mayonnaise sandwiches
into my backpack, make sure Cicatríz
is happy inside one of the side pockets
with her bony head and wet nose sticking out.

Scribble a note:

> Papi,
> Going to help the others
> so uncle DJ can live. Don't worry.
> Going to do it my way.
>
> Love,
> Canelita
>
> P.S. Cinnamon Girl.

Gonna do what you said, Papi,
gonna get my own islita, my own sky.
Gonna find those "long white stairs."
Ditch class. Ditch-ditch.

9/29/01 Saturday, Loisaida, after lunch at uncle Rummi's
cool again

Wait for Rezzy after school at her uncle's shop
by the Tanya Towers. Read the sign
Royal Robes: Used & Almost Used

Look, look, Rezzy,
show her my backpack.
It's my luggage, heh. Got a place for us.
Before she can say anything, we pick
funny-looking colored hats and shaggy clothes
from the racks. Come on, come, we gotta go
to the Cinnamon Palace.
Where, wula?
You donkey!

Pull Rezzy down the stairs
of an abandoned building on Avenue D, down, down
the cellar, way down past smoky ashes, beer bottles
of urine, and baby mice. Okeh, okeh, we'll clean it up.
Everything is going to be cool again.

Down
we go.

9/30/01 Sunday, late night, at the Cinnamon Palace
playa boricua

See my bed?

Show Rezzy, a crumpled roll
of newspapers, cardboard pillows, Mamá's *rebozo*
and a fancy old velvet blanket of palm trees
and parrots, just like uncle DJ said, life is a *playa boricua*,
a Puerto Rican beach.
And we got food, Rezzy.

Light another candle in the cellar.
See this little shoebox. Thass our dining
room table and see here inside this box, there's
cheese and crackers, candy and some
soda cans, oh, and bread, got lots of bread,
thass our refrigerator.
Come, Rezzy, sit, sit, just wait a minute.
Okeh, I know what you're thinking,
Wula, this is not a bedroom! Okeh, okeh, right?
Wait, look.

Cup my hand and scrape it against
the floor and hold it up next to the candles
by my bed.

See?
What?

Closer!
What? Dirt?

You can't see it?
Here open your hand, Rezzy.

Let me pour it on you. Now?
It feels so fine. Wula. What is it, Yo'?

Looks like dust, huh?
Kinda silvery, huh?

It's the voices, Rezzy.
It's all the voices.

They came flying down the stairs of every
city building after the Twin Towers

came crashing and then they hit bottom.
Thass why they talk to me. Thass why we are here,
Rezzy, are you listening? We are going
to put them back where they will rest,
back where uncle DJ fell too, okeh,
repeat after me okeh—

Down the long white stairs in the night
all the falling voices you will cure of fright . . .

Down the long white stairs in the night
all the falling voices you will cure of fright . . .

Give Rezzy some school sandwich bags
from Mamá's kitchen and an empty shoebox.
These are little apartments
for the voicedust, okeh, okeh, I say

Uncle Beto!
Uncle DJ!

Squint through the dust still flowering
gray in the cellar.
Where are you? In what mouth or cave or bodega

of cinders and concrete?
Why do I call him? Stupid, huh?

Donde estás? Where?
Breathe. I breathe.

Never
thought about
breathing.
It is like beginning something.
New.

In the cellar, gray light.
Gray walls.

The halls
at school are gray too.
The floors shine, wave
and then
they dissolve.

Down-down we go.
Cellar of shredded leaves
rivers, forgotten explosive oceans, Rezzy and me

laughing and swimming
holding hands. Remembering
just a few seconds ago
when we were
thirteen.

Kneel like tía Gladys on the hospital floor,
it makes me feel like I am with uncle DJ
in some weird way. Scoop, scoop the voicedust
with our hands, scoop, Rezzy sings, a little nervous,

Come little voices,
come little ones,
we are taking you back home,
come now, come.

10/1/01 Monday, late night, at the Cinnamon Palace
ballet

Yo',
we got two hundred and seventy
little voicedust baggies
in shoeboxes now! Smiles
with circles under her eyes.

Red rings
around her lips from drinking too many
cherry sodas.
Yo', are you listening to me, wula?
You know uncle Rummi is probably going crazy
wondering where I am too, you know?
He's probably saying, Where is that fatty-girl!
That's what he calls me. Where's that baby-barrel?
When are you going to lose all that pudding?
In America girls have thin necks like swans,
that's why ballet is so beautiful. And it's not *belly*,
it's ballet, can you pronounce that, Rezan, let me hear
you say ballet, now! He gives me a candy,
Here, learn with a sweet.

I see Rezzy's eyes grow shadows and her
lips stretch into wispy waves, smeared and jerky.
Rezzy slumps down on our cardboard bed.
Bows her head and sighs. Drags to the corner

of the cellar with a candle and slides down
to the floor. Scoops voices. A rat scurries into a pile
of rotten rags smashed like brains.

I don't want to go out anymore, Yo'.
She says shaking her head.
Okeh, okeh, Rez.
Hold her hand. Okeh.

You cannot show your face
You cannot leave a trace . . .
I say to myself.

I know what we'll do, Rez.
Take her hand and lift her up
and swing her around our palace
as if we are dancing ballet—
Glide across the stone stage. Fly.

From now on, Rezzy
we'll trade places. I'll be you.
And you'll—be me. *Me.*
Me?

10/2/01 Tuesday, evening, Loisaida on to Broadway
fades

After we run home
from Sister Lopez's Tarot Card Shoppe
Rezzy pastes on a tight halter top and pounds
herself into a pair of pink gypsy bell-bottoms.
Gotta be like you, Yo', right and you like me?
I wrap a thick cloth around my belly and put
on an extra pair of pants. Wear serious shoes.
All I need is a pinafore, heh, I tell her,
Heh.

Yeh, this way nobody will know us.
And we can know everybody, Rezzy, yeh.
Jus' like Sister Lopez said—
You cannot show your face.

You cannot show your face,
Rezzy copies and licks a PowerBar.
Not going to eat, Yo', this way
I'll lose all the pudding—like a swan.
Gonna get on a Zoney diet! She laughs.
What? Rezzy sucks on an orange and squirts
my eyes. Laughs. You donkey.

Shuts her eyes, makes a face
of a naughty bus driver, lets a seed roll off
her chalky-white tongue.

Stop posing! We have stuff to do.
Rezzy freezes. Her face
drops the smiles. Silence. Only the dust seems
to say things—*Hurry! Hurry!*

We both bounce up,
spin around our
cardboard boxes and folded clothes
on the floor. Except we switch clothes
and sides of the bed.

Stuff more baggies into our backpacks.
Come, Rezzy, we have a ways to go.
Hold her hand and walk upstairs.
Climb and peek outside the Cinnamon Palace.

Jump a bus.
Pass Maiden Street and Broadway.
A fireman
on a high crane shoots water

into a blue-gray box of wires and torn concrete.
Clock on a storefront
stutters and starts. Things are on
and off. In between there is strange static.
Like when the TV breaks
and the channels forget how to speak
and where to aim. Hear sirens.
Sniff, sniff, something's on fire.
It is the earth, I can't explain it,
Rezzy answers weird.

We scoop voicedust
from the bus seats, scoop more dust.
Scoop.

Rezzy turns her head, in a daze,
slowly, as if looking for something
that used to be there, like a deli or a little dog,
but she can't find it now.
I can't explain it, she repeats.
I open my backpack
and pick a few poems out of my cereal box.
These poems are about you, Rezzy,
I tell her to cheer her up a little. Listen.

ᗰᙡ

e dge

Rezzy flies me
a note in
hot orange
ink:

Guess what, Yo'?
I am going on a Zoney diet.
Just chicken and pastrami,
wula! Pulls a beaded strand of hair
down to her dark lips. She looks
sooo cute. Her eyes blink fast
and her smooth skin is sweaty sweet.

September 1, 01

rezzy scrapes off her fingernail polish

then she scrapes a scab in her head
in between her braids, under her baseball cap
she tastes the blood on her finger
tastes like bacon she says,

scratches her elbow, giggles,
then her armpit. She listens to
the Dixie Chicks. At St. Mark's, we sit
on the stairs with Cicatríz and stare at the guys
coming to a poetry reading—
ooooh, uuuuh. blah.

September 3, 01

stick out my
tongue at rezzy

Trace my hand
on a blank sheet of paper
five squiggly candles
five soft towers of heat
five ways of talking at the same time
to five friends—

Rezzy,
Alma & Carmela (they're always together)
Jenikajade &
McKenzie.

September 6, 01

Rezzy coughs, sniffs the air,
bites her crunchy fingernails.
Get off at the Cinnamon Palace
where we started.
Let's sneak to the hospital to see uncle DJ!
I ask her. Can't, Yo', just can't.

I am going back
home to see uncle Rummi.
She empties
her backpack of dustvoices, piles them into mine.
I'm in enough trouble as it is, wula!
Leaves with her head droopy.
She whistles funny and fades.
Rezzy fades.

10/3/01 Wednesday, F train to Coney Island, night
halloween

Hey—Moondraggin'?
Is that you?

Dressed up for Halloween,
Ain't that weeks from now? WashUdoin'?

A blurry boy calls me leaning on the door
to the Cinnamon Palace.

You gettin' chopped? Look like
you been smokin' the pipe. Bugged out yet?
Why you wearin' Rezan's rags?
You're out of it, man! Haven't seen ya'
at school. Remember me? Hey . . . it's just me
Zako, at your service, as they say.

His smooth weasel voice. I remember.
So what are you? A witch? A scarecrow?
Grabs the coil of shirts rolled around my waist.
Spins me—to him. You from California, huh?

Nah, I say, Puertoricans are from here.
You be one crazy girl. Total wack.

Zako lights up and says as he puffs,
Come . . .
on . . .
portee . . .
reecan . . .

I'm a smokareecan.
You don't know nothing, do ya'?
He tells me and gives me a mean look.
I notice a bruised bump
on his forehead from long ago,
underneath his skin, a torn cloud,
a falling flag.

Hunch my shoulders like Rezzy
and say nothing. My chest doesn't move.
I don't know where my breath goes.

*Maybe after a while you don't need
to breathe, huh, uncle DJ, I whisper. Huh?*

Come on, Rezan, oops, I mean, Rezzy,
Wait, wait, hold it, excuse me, I mean,
Zako jokes and laughs—
Yo'. That's your name, isn't it?
Yolandah . . . huh. You and me got the same trip.
Everyone calls me Zako. But they don't really
know my name. I mean, my for-reals name.
It's Zacarías.

Can you say it?
Za-ca-rías . . . Zac . . .
Shhh . . . Just say once.

Thass right, Yolandah. Promise
never to tell Marietta or anybody, eh?
Yolandah . . . you listening or what!

My name's not Yolandah.
My name's not Rezan. It's not me
or you or we or this or that or what!

Man, you're so chopped, Porteereecan.
Porteereecan? Thass not my name either.
What-what did you say?

My name is *noche*—night,
You can't touch it, you think you see it
but you can't. That's what these clothes
are made of—black
nightdust.

I say things to get out of things
but I just get tangled up and tired, uncle DJ.
So tired. But I can't let him know
what I'm doing. Can't let him know
about the voices asleep
in their little baggie-beds downstairs
in the Palace. Gotta get him away from here
so he won't find out. Hear me, uncle DJ?

Man, you are loaded—mumbling
to yourself and all that. Come on,
Yolandah . . . I'll show you how
to get really high.
Okeh, okeh,
I say through a hole
in my head into another hole
in the streets.

We take the F train
to the last stop. Grabs my hand,
Welcome to my island. Zako says
with a long skinny voice.
Welcome to Coney Island, dude.
Take a hit!
Zako pops
his short pipe into my mouth.

Maybe if I smoke a little I can rest.
Maybe if I loosen up a bit
I can breathe, maybe,
like I used to
in the sweet winds of Iowa.

In . . .

                out . . .

In   . . . in . . .

In.

The night sky squirms
        neon cobras
                blue-fire snakes, pink
                        dragons on
                                old women faces
                                        flamey makeup
                                                look at
                                        their narrow
                                                wasp-
                                                waists
                                                like
                                                sucking
                                        on a tube
                                of mustard, sad-eyed
                        girls flap
                their hair
        hot lipstick gloss
and candy hairspray
        sticks to the air
                                        they scream
                                                they sing
                        the dahk-dahk of darts
                                and a thousand ant people
        down below

                    bubble in circles around me
                                             but it
                                                   is only
me
                                       and Zako
                up way up
                                  in a painted metal cage
                            crazy cars and faces
            crashing

                                              in space.

Been on the Zyklone before?
Zako asks me. It's like a giant hungry
dumb lizard. Wish it would come rolling
down, dude, on top of the world!
Zako squeals into a shovel of air
pouring over our faces.

You hear me, Yoland . . . I mean, uh . . .
Call me Yo', okeh. I tell Zako,
trying to shake off the hot-cold wires
buzzin' and snappin' in my head.

Take a deep-deep breath. But it gets
jammed up in my nose. Wish I could see
Puerto Rico, like uncle DJ says:
Una playa boricua will cure you for life!

All I see is black waves, flashes
and watery-dots, and sharp streaks thin
as hairs. A giant flat clock by the moon.
Almost midnight.

Make up a story
In my head—barely breathing—

Bet mamá Mercedes sits by uncle DJ
and pull-pulls her pomegranate-colored rosary
from herself. Where is my Yolanda María?
She's asking. She's been gone for three days!
It's her manda, she's pulling. Just as I am
spinning my manda here in the air.
She rubs each bead as if it was
a seed, a river, she presses it
as if it was a mountain,
a machete from Cidra,
as if she was holding her father's hand

across the oceans, as if he never forgot her
so far away waving adios
leaning on a small wooden *bohío* in Caguas,
thick green leaves
at his feet and the violin voice of the *coquí* frog
in the blue-green night air. Papi Reinaldo
rolls over on his side of the hospital room.
Mamá kisses uncle DJ's hand *buenas noches*,
then sits back in her own small frame
and closes her eyes, her lips open
with my name again and again and her
hands shaky. Mamá?

All I see are the gooey heads
of Zako and Rezzy exploding
puff-puffing the night smoke,
gettin' chopped, gettin' loaded,
next to me. Sucking in, in, in, then—

Zako wraps his arms around Rezzy.
Lisssen to the ocean, he says
with his teeth out. He smears his
face against her cheek,
Come here, lisssen. He pushes her head down

into his shirt. For a moment, I see Rezzy
with Zako, she looks up and asks him,
Aren't you going out with Marietta?

But, it isn't Rezzy I am looking at.
Me. It's only me
afraid and shattered.

10/4/01 Thursday, Avenue D, Loisaida, dawn
flamenco

Slouch on a pile of gypsy clothes
on the floor of the Palace. Rezzy gone.
Where did she go?

My head's wired, tight. Gotta keep
the voices calm. Under my pillow. Some
in my China chinelas, my Chinese slippers.
Heh-heh. Laugh a little through
my lips. Chinachinelas. Heh-heh. So bugged out.
But . . . gotta save the voices.

Zakooo, I say with
my mouth dry going slower than the words.
Help meee, save-save
voicesssss.

Zako stares into the wall,
talks to himself, weaving a web
of cutouts, words torn in half that don't mean
nothing.

He lays down and whimpers and almost cries
by the gray-blue stairs in the hot loud morning.
His cries drip into the ash and slice into the hairs
on my arms.
Itchy, itchy.

Rip out papers from my backpack, hold on,
a neat brick of letters from the cereal box, heh-heh,
maybe if I read them, I can go to sleep, heh,
just for a little while, heh . . . and when I wake up
Zako will be gone and
Rezzy will be back . . .

∾

July 12, 00

Dear uncle DJ,

It's sooo hot in Iowa. And muggy. I am still not used to it.
I remember the first thing Mamá and me did when we got
here from New York—this is embarrassing—
was stop at a gas station and go to the bathroom. Guess
what was growing on the corner by the gas pumps?

Corn! Papi said, No matter where we go, the earth
makes miracles. I dunno, heh. Here's a postcard
of the Amana Colonies—whatever that is. Bye.

Love con papayas,
Your only niece.
Y

August 25, 00

Dear uncle DJ,

School started last Monday.
West Liberty, Iowa . . . heard of it?
My school is sooo-sooo old! Longfellow School.
No middle school, no elementary—
we're all piled up like masa!
And the town is as small as my backpack. One main
street, one theater and one Mexican restaurant. Lots of
Mexicans, at least, Papi said—at least there's somebody
I can talk to. Sure. I just get on the phone and talk to all
my friends, well, a couple. This place sucks.

Adios arroz,
Love con plátanos,
YO'

P.S. Mamá wants to go to an antique shop.
What's that? By the way it is West Liberty,
not West Liver. Ha!

March 27, 01

Dear uncle DJ,

Papi says that if I want to go to San Francisco—
he calls it San Pancho—I have to get good grades.
Lately, he's been calling me matraca or maraca or
something like that because I am always dancing
and singing in our house or talking on the phone.
Did I tell you I have lots of boy friends?
Gotta run—in the rain.

Love con mambo,
Canela

P.S. Do you Hip-Hop?

Dear uncle DJ,

Totally bored. Booored. Booored!
How do you say bored in Spanish? I should ask Mamá.
Borro? Sounds like burro! Mamá's always reading books
from Bell's Used Book Store and newspapers in
Spanish that she gets from Tía and even in English
even though she only went to third grade back
in Aguas Buenas. But she needs to work out. Maybe,
I'll take her to the Field House in Iowa City—
it's a really cool gym by the river. They even have a
running track above the basketball court, near the ceiling.
Went there last weekend with my friend Miguela. Well,
that's what Mr. Rolodex calls her at school. My name is SKY,
she tells everyone. She's the *más güapa* girl in the world.
Sky's white as the moon and has pure black long hair
like a dark waterfall, all the way down to her butt
and all the guys at Longfellow are crazy about her.
And guess what? She gets everything she wants
without ever saying a word. Chévere, huh?
She's like a mystery goddess.

Love con chili fries
and chili beans,
Y

P.S. Am I a mystery goddess too? Dunno.

April 9, 01

Dear Canelita,

I called you last night. Where's everybody?
So, I am sending you this letter express,
if that's possible in the Mission District.
Your tía Aurelia is very ill.
She's got pneumonia. Poor old señora.
Gladys took her to emergency at St. Luke's last night.
I was playing at the Galería de la Raza on
Twenty-fourth street for an AIDS benefit. When
I got home no one was there. Now, you guys.
What's happening? But, don't worry. And tell
my sister Mercedes that everything is going to be ok.
I hope. Light a *veladora*. And call me.

Love con familia,
Your tío Beto

April 25, 01

Dear Canelita,

What's going on in your head?
Last night when we talked you sounded like, well,
like your words were all knocking against each other.
Your voice was all sloppy. Have you been drinking?
Tía Aurelia is getting worse, I think. She's hooked up
to a machine, a blue hose taped across her mouth. Just
opens her eyes and nods when I talk to her. Gladys says
that as soon as they get her off the *máquina* she will speak
a mile a minute. My chest feels like a slab of concrete,
heavy, sad and numb at the same time. Gotta get back
to Loisaida. But, I am still giggin'. It helps me forget
about the little white room full of hoses and machines
and the smell of Jergen's Lotion and mashed
whoknowswhat kinda food inside plastic bags and IVs.
I hope I am wrong about you.
Yeah, I probably am. Forgive me.
It's all in my head, *ando esbaratao'*. I am falling apart here.

Lov4U,
Uncle DJ

☾☽

Still can't go to sleep.
Zako's mumbling faster.

☾☽

April 14, 01

Dear uncle DJ,

Like I said on the phone a couple days ago,
I went out with my friends. Well, I was with Sky.
And I don't know where Mamá and Papi were.
Whatever, dunno. Me and Sky went to the 620 Club
in Iowa City. Really cool place. Sky goes all the time.
It's for teens. Nobody knows Hip-Hop around here.
And they play music and we crack up. I hope
tía Aurelia is feeling better. Got two candles going.
Love for Tía,
Y

P.S. Sky says it doesn't matter if I am
a Puertorican because she is a Mexiowan.

∞

Shhh. What was that?
Don't know what's going on.
Can't tell if it's a letter I am hearing
Or a voice made of dust.

∞

April 20, 01

Dear Canelita,

What's happening to you?

This morning your mamá was crying on the phone.
She doesn't know what to do with you?
Why didn't you tell me you've been coming home so late?
At four in the morning? This thing with Sky.
Remember what Tía says—
Dime con quien andas, y te diré quien eres.
If you hang out with losers, you're a loser too.
Don't know what to tell you. Feel like you lied to me.

You said you didn't know where your mother
and father were last week. They were looking
The 620 is a bar, *puro bochinche,* just a craz
your mamá said. Please think about what you
Can't believe it. I am very hurt. I wish your fat
would speak up. I hate doing this.

Love always,
Uncle Beto

P.S. The doctor says tía Aurelia will be ok, *ber*
in about ten days. We're gonna get back to No
soon after that. I visit her in the hospital when
I can. Maybe, should visit more often.

∞

Uncle DJ, where are you?
Feels like you are right here.

∞

๑

What if uncle DJ woke up?
What would I tell him?
How could I talk about all this?

๑

April 29, 01

Dear uncle DJ,

I guess I messed up—but it was my birthday.
Thirteen! Didn't even get a card! Mamá and Papi,
they're so out of it. I mean, we don't celebrate anything.
Go to church and take walks, that's all. Or they talk about
the old days. Papi tells the story about the nights in Caguas
when he would dive in the waters under a full moon
for the 100th time.
And Mamá says she was better off *en la islita,*
en el batey bajo el cielo or she goes on about *el Parque
de las Palomas en San Juan*, the Flamboyan trees and the
water springs in Coamo. Embarrassing. Then she says
"Aqui en América, things are betta." Makes my head feel

like a roller coaster. Anyway, here kids go to bars and they don't ask for IDs. It's not like New York. And Sky is cool, she looks out for me. You know? And this boy I just met, Cheyenne, he's so cool too. Well, he's a runaway from Oxford in Pennsylvania. On his way to California. Can you believe that? Mamá made him *pollo frito con habichuelas*. Yesterday. Cheyenne's really a nice boy and *bien güapo*. He's not mean or bad. He told me a lot of his secrets, just like Sky. We are all tight friends. Cheyenne was showing Sky and me how to hitchhike last night, on the road to Iowa City. You know, like, how to tell if the driver is alright or if he's a weirdo, you know, *a paquetero*. Cheyenne says he's been to Miami too!

Love,
Canela

P.S. Hurry up, summer!

Where does this letter go?

୭୭

Dear uncle DJ,

When are you going to start that RadioSabor
tía Gladys talks about? Last night on the phone
she said that you want to build a radio studio
on the tenement roof back in Alphabet City.
I don't know if that's what she said. All the words
are swirling in my head like Mamá's *asopao'*.
There's so much to tell you. Mamá wants me to go out
with one of my class friends, Dana Barlow, you know
her dad teaches at Grinnell College, in the African American
Studies Program. Sometimes we do our homework
assignments in Iowa City. Go to visit the bookstores and
bum around too. I'd rather be with Sky. If Papi lets me.
He's so grouchy. I wish he had a real job. Everything
is chickens and turkeys for him. Can you believe that.
He says he's going to make *mole mexicano* for
Thanksgiving. That means he's going to swing that animal
around by the neck like a lasso and slap it on the porch
wall like he slams chickens. Sick. And he says that
God put turkeys on earth for us to eat. Oh. Excuse me.

He's so gross and embarrassing. Maybe I'll become
a vegetarian. Sky's a vegetarian. But, what will I eat?
Oh, that's Sky tapping at my window. Bye.

Love con moondust,
Canelita

April 17, 01

Dear uncle DJ,

Maybe's Papi's right, I am a maraca.
I don't have time to write poems anymore. Mamá
just lays around all day and says, *Tengo hoflash*,
I am so hot, hotty-hot! And fans herself with both hands,
as if she's got little chicken wings instead of fingers.
Sóbame con alcohol, rub my neck with alcohol, rub
my back, get the *ruda*. Then make her *te de yerba buena*
for her stomach. *Tráeme el mentolato*, Get the VapoRub,
so she swallows it! Ugh! And what's a hoflash? Mamá
says it's like *el desarollo* for me when I get my period,
but for her it's *el cambio*. I don't get it. I might as well
open a *botica*! Then she talks about the new Mexican

restaurant right across from the Strand theater where
she says she has a good chance of getting a job. Sure.
And Papi, he's always at the chicken *factoría* or with
his friends drinking beers under a tree by the *colmado*
or betting on *gallos*. When Sky can't come
over there's nothing to do. So, I go window shopping
and walk the four blocks of the city. Over and over.
There isn't a store sale I haven't seen. Baseball gloves are
sixty dollars! Can you believe that? This Saturday there is
a Watermelon Jubilee in Conesville a few miles south.
And Casey's Tenderloin Burgers which is run by a
Vietnamese woman has a twofer special on Fridays.
Twofers are when you get two for one. I hate this place.
Well, the only things that I do like are the cicadas in
the trees and the fields. They have electric bellies
and are as big as walnuts, they're purple with fuzzy
eyelashes. And they sing in secret extraterrestrial
languages. At night, they rule the planet. You can't
see them but everything is dripping with their sound,
their violin songs. Chévere, huh?

Love con cicadas,
Canelita

April 18, 01

Dear uncle DJ,

Just want to tell you that you are the only one
I can talk to. Hope you like this card. I drew it
with all my favorite colors. Sky blue, emerald
green and wicked ruby red, red like Mamá's purses
and scarves and hats. My favorite is sky blue.
Did you know that the sky above your head is
the purest blue, an infinite ocean of sky upon
sky. And the sky farthest from you is a milky-way sky,
a sky mixed with the rainy clouds, a faint see-through sky.

Am I an artist, uncle DJ?

Love con marimas,
Canela

April 26, 01

Dear Canela,

Your tía Aurelia is doing much better at home.
Just left her and Gladys watching a *telenovela* this
afternoon. Went straight to the Muni Pier next to Cannery
Row, well, that's just a name for the tourist trap by the
Wharf. Went all the way to the end of the pier, past the
crab-netters and an old Chinese woman fishing up an
eel. Turned to the City and guess what I heard bouncing
through the waves from the concrete benches of
Aquatic Park? Guess.

Amor del mar,
Uncle DJ

P.S. Be good. Pray for tía Aurelia.

April 30, 01

Dear uncle DJ,

Sky says you heard someone jump into the water
to save a baby from a great white shark.
Just kidding. Dunno.
It's kinda cold here. Heard of "freezing rain"? Sky tells me
in the winter it's like glass everywhere.

Was it firecrackers?

Love con ice congas and snowball guayavas,
Canela

P.S. Isn't the Muni Pier where Mamá and Papi met?
What's Aquatic Park, a place to park your pools?
Did you know that I keep all your letters
in a cereal box that Papi gave me? Under my bed.

May 3, 01

Dear Firecracker Canelita,

Yeah, my sister met your dad at the pier.
Ain't that a wild one. A Puertorican from the Big Apple
visiting the City and a Puertoriqueña straight off
the island staring at Alcatraz. ¡Bendito!

Love con Mexican salsa,
Uncle DJ

May 7, 01

Dear Canela,

Contestant number three?

Ready with your answer?
Please press the correct button! Ha!
It wasn't some guy or a shark or
a circus juggler throwing balloons
into the water. Come on, nena.

Use your maraca. I'll tell you.
There was a row of *congero* brothers
sitting on a little theater facing the sea,
they call it Aquatic Parque and man,
they were blowing sofrito with their souls,
puro tumbao'—in front of the ocean,
now that's what I call a Puerto Rican symphony.

Love con bongo magic,
Uncle DJ

P.S. Like this postcard, the cable cars?

May 13, 01

Dear Yolanda,

Tía Aurelia is home now, in her little hotel room with her
window facing Mission Street. Watching the *jevos* passing
by the junkies all strung out. Man, wish I could get her out
of here. Went to look for a place for her in Noe Valley. $800.
For a square box with a carpet and a heater. That's it.
Almost as bad as Loisaida. At least it had a heater.

Problem is all she's got is my uncle Ismael's pension check.

Please call or write me right now.

Stop whatever you are doing and send me a little note. Hurry.

Maybe you can come and help your tía Gladys while I find tía Aurelia a cozy place.

Did you get my letter about Aquatic Parque?

Love from this island to yours—on a windy day.

Uncle DJ

May 20, 01

Dear Canelita,

Why don't you answer my letters, the phone?

Your mom says she hasn't seen you in four days.

What's going on? She says you're not at school either.

Just when I need you, nena. Please, por favor, answer.

Your uncle who never forgets you,

DJ Roberto

‍

Breathe a little whimper,
read this letter
over and over again:

May 25, 01

Dear Canela,

I have an idea.
Why don't you come back to New York,
all of you? We just got in from San Francisco.
At last. Tía said, *ya vayanse*, can you believe it?
She told us to get out. But I got her a visiting nurse.
Look, the Lower East Side is about sixteen hours from
Iowa, plus a skip and a mambo! Just a little *apretao'* in the
Everything Room. Maybe it's time we all got back together,
our tenement will be our islita. Please get back to me.

Mucho love con () () ()
Your uncle Beto, DJ

P.S. You'll help build my radio station up on the roof?
RadioSabor FM, okay? And you can write poems there too.
Bring that old cereal box you've been keeping since
you were a little girl. Just you and nobody else.
Hurry, write, call. Chéverechévere!

∾

My heart beats low-low and
an icy sweat covers me. Sniff, sniff,
Zako says if I take another hit
I'll feel more energy. Zako.
Something in the pipe
makes my eyes stay open forever.
Nothing—my nose hurts. I fill my pockets
with voicedust as Zako talks-talks. Got to save
the voices. Got to carry them back
to Ground Zero. My manda. It is my manda.

Want to eat a whole
row of soda crackers and a little white pan
of cheese dip, root beer. Chew gum. Want to
but can't. Just can't.
My stomach feels tight

and burns too. Heh, almost like salsa.
Wipe my face.

Like I see little wings with
the sides of my open eyes. I snatch them,
dust, feathers, mosquitos, heh-heh, mosquitos,
white mosquitos, little armies that will lead me
out upstairs. Heh. My back hurts kinda. Don't
know if it's my back or my stomach or
my heart. So empty,
heh, the morning light spills on the stairs like milk.

Sneak out.
Crawl with Cicatríz. Wind
cradle me. Wind-wind
from all around the world.

Out here now
where everyone can hear, lissen—

I notice the stars
for the first time, chewing pieces of the sky.
Can you hear them, Cicatríz?
They are waiting for you.

Notice the little songs of people
moving quiet in the wee hours of the morning.
Hear that, Cicatríz? They are all saying
that you are the most beautiful girl in the world.
They are saying they love you and that they
will never forget you.
A woman prays, see how she looks away
and lowers her head inside a scarf and that man
asleep while he's holding a lunch bag.
See that, Cicatríz? He has your favorite *bacalaitos*.
Just you and me now, Cicatríz.
Here, if I can't have the crackers
you can have them, here
try a little cheese dip, wipe it off
your nose after you finish, okeh,
okeh, now, be careful, the mosquitos,
and the feet, see those feet, watch
them, they're sneaky feet, don't
follow them, follow me, Cicatríz, come
and remember, always, we can't
lose those little gray baggies, okeh,
okeh, now, gonna put you back
into your little apartment, right
here in my backpack, here's a little

cookie, the last one, wish I had some,
let's go now, come, come
and shhh . . . shhhhh don't you say a word
to anyone, until uncle DJ comes home,
ready, okeh, okeh, let's go, nobody's
gonna see me, they're gonna think
I am some kinda Mexican gypsy,
Spanish, a Flamenco dancer, yeh-yeh,
let's go and catch up with Rezzy.

Wait
until the sun comes up. Wait
by PS 1486. Pace back and forth,
look mean into the street where
a bicycle man floats by like an angel.

hot pink note

Let's follow Rezzy
to Mrs. Camacho's class, heh.
Look at her walk fast-fast
up the stairs. Is she running away
from us, Cicatríz? Or maybe,
she thinks she sees me
in the crowd, huh? Maybe,
we should go home, I should
wash the dishes, bet you the sink
is so dirty, no one there, everyone
at the hospital. Dunno.

Uncle DJ
can you hear me? Why don't you
say something? Why don't you answer?
There's too much dust to clean.
Uncle DJ?

Even here in the janitor room
by the brown mop and yellow

117

plastic bucket there is too much dust.
I am gonna pinch your nose, Cicatríz,
so you won't smell the ammonia,
and plug your ears so you won't
hear all the dustvoices.

The bell rings-rings
and Rezzy passes me.
Hey—
drops me a hot pink note.

> Police come to class
> looking for you.
> Meet me tomorrow at five thirty.
> Sister Lopez's Tarot Card Shoppe.
> Later.
>
> —Rezzy

10/6/01 Saturday, nodding off on Avenue D, muggy afternoon
my razor

Come, Cicatríz,
let's hang by our old place.
Get some fresh clothes,
some cookies. We're not
going back until we save all
the voices, remember. We made
a manda. Shhhh, shhhh, up
the stairs, second floor, third,
okeh, okeh.

Sniff, sniff, smells like
pasteles, or maybe someone's
frying pork chops next door, mmmmm.
Okeh, the door's open, a little.

Must be Papi, he's always forgetting,
huh, Cicatríz, are you listening to me?

Tiptoe,
tip-tip, tiptoe. Is that

Papi leaning over the sink
reading something by the light?

It's probably a Wanted Picture.
You know, like on the milk carton,
the little kids. You know I am not
a little kid, Cicatríz, wonder what
he's reading.

Better hide in the closet
by my sofa-room, where tía Gladys
keeps her work clothes. Let's see.
Wait, hear that?

ᙥ

House made of sofrito
So many moons and dreams
Aguas Buenas, Cayey, Puerto Rico
Papi and me dance outside
How funny life seems.

July 13, 01

Papi's reading one
of my poems.
What's Papi reading now?

Under the Flamboyan
In my heart
There is a little girl
A flower from the start . . .
Come to my arms, Canela
Are you safe,
Where are you sleeping?
Wake up, wake up, nena,
I am so alone, weeping.

Papi, Papi, heh.
Is that your poem? I almost say
through the crack in the door.

Papi pops his arm
and looks at his watch.
I almost forgot, he whispers,

they're taking Beto off the ventilator thing
to see if he can breathe on his own.

Uncle DJ?
Uncle DJ, wait. I am not ready.
I, uh, uh, I, uh, I still need to save the voices.
I want to come see you, but, I am not finished . . .
don't know . . .

Papi dashes out without saying
another word.

What shall we do, Cicatríz?
I switch on the light in the tiny closet.

Check my miniature watch.
Rezzy's waiting for me, but
I want to see uncle DJ too.

Grab the zebra boa from Tía's clothes rack
and the blouse with circle mirrors.

In every mirror
there is a wavy pool

with two dark sad eyes
looking down.

Meet Rezzy at Sister Lopez's shoppe.
No one there except
Sister Lopez who's sitting down
petting her rough black cat, on
the phone talkin' in a low voice, something
about *Is he ok?*

Wonder where Rezzy is?
Wonder what's going on
at the hospital? Where will I stay tonight?
Zako's still at the Palace or
is he with RGB or Marietta?

I don't want to smoke that stuff, makes my head
get wired and then I laugh out loud-loud
and then I can't close my eyes.

It's laced with some good stuff, Zako says.
Gettin' chopped keeps things smoooth.

Sniff, sniff.
Cicatríz pokes her nose through
some butter-colored candles.
Yolanda, did you save all the voices?
A husky voice crackles.
Where did you go lookin', muchacha?

Down the long white stairs in the night
All the falling voices you will cure of fright
You cannot show your face
You cannot leave a trace
Do this with all your heart and all your might
And your uncle will rest in the highest place.

Sister Lopez walks up to me slow-slow,
she looks kinda smaller all of a sudden,
with her arms out as if about to ask for rain
from the rufeh, as if about to lift up
an invisible tray of flowers to someone
that just died, her virgensita almost hidden.
She hugs me
and presses her face against my shoulder.

Rezan is not coming, Sister Lopez says, touching my face.
She called, said they're going back home to Kuwait.
Someone gassed their store!

Run-run, run,
then I think of nothing.
Drag
slow
to
Royal Robes

FDNY
Ashes and smoke.

A charred pile
of steel hangers and smoke-spotted walls.
More smoke and black soot figures.
Torn half faces, clouds and
a beehive of embers.

A couple of strangers take a picture.
Think of Iowa. Sky. Sky, can you hear me?
Can you see me? When will this end?

Rezzy glances at me from the crowd—
she's still wearing
my black tights and denim jacket.
We are not terrorists, uncle Rummi
says, ducking the photographers, Now I go back
to Kuwait, no business, no life here no more,
Everything lost. All lost.

Rezzy stares hard,
takes off my jacket, drops it on the sidewalk,
I almost disappear,

like miles away and I touch her
through the small window in the taxi
and she touches me.
Says something with her face against
the glass, but uncle Rummi pulls her
away.

I stand
alone again.

She's gone. Rezzy without light.
Sky, where are you?

Uncle DJ . . . can you hear me?
Will you leave me too?
Gone, all gone.
Kick-kick away
my old funky blue-black jacket.

Rezzy, Rezzy, I say.
Rez-zy—her name
gets stuck
in my throat.
A razor. But it's
my razor.

10/7/01 Sunday, alone on the rufeh, Loisaida, 3 am
love congas

Take a shot
of Peppermint Schnapps,
tuck the bottle from Shorty's bodega
in my backpack. Spit it back out.

Cicatríz, better not lick this bottle
bad for you, bad! Slouch down Avenue C
back to my old building, look up at the third floor.
Lights out. Cover my mouth and face with
Mamá's Hindu shirt. Rest the bottle down
on the fire hydrant in front of the stoop.
Sit.

Climb the stairs.
First floor, second floor, go to the rufeh.
See the busted wires and the trash bags.
RadioSabor in a heap of beer bottles
and trash.

Sing a little tune by J.Lo.
Sit on a milk crate, sing a little tune.

Gaze at the washed flat hot sky,
crooked, shaky
and empty in my chest.

Rub my neck
feel a wart by my vein.

Pick a letter
in my backpack, from my cereal box.
Strike a match and read.

ოთ

June 3, 01

My Canelita,

I called and called you last night but your mom said
you are not in the mood to talk to anyone. I am
so sorry about your friend, Sky.
Wish I could hug you mucho.
When my papa died, *en paz descanse*, I didn't
know what hit me. I told myself, It's like he just
isn't here anymore. Didn't feel a thing, I was sixteen,

three years older than you. The sheriff came to our
apartamento at midnight, handed Mamá a letter and said, I
am sorry. Didn't even visit him in the hospital, I just didn't,
didn't want to see him without legs, the diabetes had
eaten him all up, when he passed I remembered his
words, *La vida es un sueño y los sueños sueños son.*
Can you read Spanish? Life is a dream and dreams are
merely dreams. And, Canelita, I was always a dreamer.

Loisaida is beautiful. It's so good to be back home.
Hearing from you will make it perfecto. Please call
or write me, sooner.

Your tío Beto, DJ

P.S. Here's a hug (). And three more ()()().
They look like congas,
Love Congas. ()()()()()

☺☺

Crush
the letter into a spiked white carnation of nothing.

Pick the letter
I keep folded inside a little red silk pouch.

ᕯ

June 13, 01

Dear uncle Beto, DJ Beto

Dunno. Words happen
at strange times. This feels like a poem
but it is full of *lágrimas*, tears.

Sky said
the winter nights in Iowa
are the best in the world. Like electric
moondust from heaven.
We walked for about an hour
north from West Liberty
away from the tiny houses and trailers
and the one theater that wets the town with orange
haloes on the streets and buildings. It was raining
and everything was so bright and quiet, still
and moving at the same time, like a video
of torn clouds and blue stars, then I felt so alone

running away from home, wanted to go back but
Sky was laying on the highway looking up straight
into the sparkles floating over us saying, "See that star,
that's mine, it's the same shape as I am when I am
dancing," and Cheyenne told her that he bet
she would chicken out before he would if
a car came down the road, cuz, he was laying
down too and I said, *no seas gallina, Miguela*,
that was Sky's real name, don't be a chicken part
I told her, then I did the same thing and we were
like three floating wet dolls on a river but it was
the asphalt on Highway 6 to Iowa City, a beer truck
peeled a sharp turn out of a warehouse and rumbled
toward us. Get up! I yelled but they were gigglin'
and holding hands, slurpin' Peppermint Schnapps,
okeh, okeh, you win, Cheyenne said as he rolled
fast to the side of the road. Sky, come on, but
Sky was laughing and stumbling on her elbows,
tell me you love me, she said,
and—can't
write anymore, uncle DJ. I can't even feel
my hand write, or my heart beat.

Canelita

☙

Scribble a poem with one eye open.

☙

this doesn't need a title

i want
to see
what is
on the other side of the d u s t

maybe
that's
where
all the dustvoices live.

maybe that's where uncle Beto
and Sky wait for me.

maybe
i
am the dust?

Dust?
Another word
for scattered dreams
in the streets.

Today & forever

෨

Take another
swig and spit-spit it out again. Then I guzzle it
like cherry soda,
spill it over my chin,
down my pants and shoes.

Cooool.

10/8/01 Monday, on the rufeh, Loisaida, 11:30 pm
drippy pizza

Climb
down
drowsy
the escape ladder and hang above by the kitchen
window, where I used to live. Bet Mamá

kneels by her little city of red candles. The razor
in my throat cuts and burns at the same time.
Hold the steel bars tight so I won't fall.

Tight-tight
so I won't feel a thing.
Maybe if I stretch I can kick up
the half open window,
I can crawl back into the Everything Room
sneak into my sofa-room and pull
my playa blankets over me.

Then, maybe if I sleep long enough
I can start over
when I wake up.

Bet Mamá is smoothing my pillows like always
and straightening out my blankets.
She always arranges my pencils, or sometimes
I catch her holding up one of my
old school class photos,
from Longfellow.

Close
my eyes. Bite my lips.

Mandas
are for
losers.

Stretch my leg, almost
to the window, uh . . .

Yo' Moondragin!
With your tongue-a-saggin'.
Whass your problem, you
playin' like a monkey on a cage?
Your friend from Kuwhat couldn't hang
with you, had to go back
to her terrorist mama, huh!

The razor burns-burns, I turn,
jerk my head down
lose my grip and slip,
slide down the ladder and
jump, roll and slam into a bag of burned sticks.
Cicatríz spins and Marietta grabs her
by the head. Comes
to me—

Marietta swishes above me
slows and snickers,

You shrimpy-bubble-brain-
buck-toothed-flat-chested loser!

She saunters
past Zako
eating a slice of
drippy pizza.

Do it! Zako shouts slurry crazy,
his tongue sticky and his eyes gone.
Do it to her!

Marietta kicks me
in the face, slow
kicks
and so fast
my right eye pops something,
hot water gushes out
of my head and squirts
in my hands.

Marietta stands over me, with her shoe
on my neck. Brings Cicatríz up to her nose.
Now tell me little dirty doggy,
tell Marietta about this skanky ho' messin' with Zako!

She keeps a hold on Cicatríz,
runs with the guys, throws Cicatríz to Zako,
runs toward Tompkins Square Park,
laughing out loud
as if the world was a piece of black dirt
under your shoes and you could shake-shake it
until it fell apart.

Heh-heh, s'ok, Cicatríz,
Just hold on, I say and push

back the swollen ball over my right eye.
Just wait, Cicatríz. We're gonna get 'em.
See Marietta? She's laying down next to you
on the grass, takin' a toke from Zako's hand
thinking I can't see her.
As soon as I catch up, heh,
I don't care
if they're waiting for me, RGB, Lil' Weez,
the other guys inside
their stupid puffed jackets.
Stumble and walk, come on, get up!
Stumble again,
I get up again,
scraped and bleeding
hot rosy glue down
one side of my face
sniff-sniff, smells like Christmas
I get up, limp-limp,
comin' to get you, girl, heh-heh,
sniff-sniff, So, so
ready.

10/9/01 Tuesday, Tompkins Square Park, midnight sharp,
Loisaida
down

One foot
ahead of the other,
make sure I keep
moving forward, heh,
okeh-okeh,

just remember, Canela,
when you step up
past the gate,
Marietta is going to jump you,
it doesn't matter, cuz
this time, it's just you
there's no one else now
just you, heh-heh

I can barely see,
the park looks like
a gray bubble moon with wiry
owls draped across a shadowy crater,
some are trapped upside down

in the branches kinda like bats, oh
my head is pounding
splinters, or is it my eye,
I can barely
see, heh, Cicatríz,
is that you?

Give me back Cicatríz!
I say, a long high voice flies out of my face—
Give her back to me!

Who's that? Who? I can't hear youuu,
Zako says in the gray light leaning on the gray tree
trunk.
A slice of skin peels by my eyebrow
over my eye.

She's
all
I
have . . .
I say standing dragging my backpack with one hand
rubbing off blood paste from my mouth
with the other.

Marietta comes up to me,
her sad painted face sharp bent downward
her mouth twitching, her nose runny, You got nothin',
you got nobody,
YolandahMoondraggin'.

Yolandamondragón!
Yolandamondragón!

I say it so fast
my fist shoots out wavy
with my words all together like lightning
so far I can see Marietta's face change
into someone old scared frozen.
Then
gray
smoke
no
sound
as

I fall.

She's out, dude. Zako says laughing barking.
I can't move. So tired, my head crackin'
my face burnin', my eye dying, but
I can still see shapes.

She didn't even touch me, she's blind as the weasel.
Marietta laughs out. Let's get outta here!
She says, licks a scratch on her arm
and they float out of the park,
Zako throws Cicatríz on the ground.
Get off me, you worm!
Coughs and follows after the group, leans
alone toward the half flames of headlights and
mixed-up sounds of morning noise.

I am laying on the grass, to one side.
A rough breeze splits the hair
on my forehead in half.

Cicatríz! Come
here, girl . . .

I thought,
I thought,

I could save all the voices,
uncle DJ.
But I couldn't. Just couldn't. I am so sorry,
uncle DJ. All I have is what's inside
my backpack. Nothin' but
dust.

The razor in my throat slices up to my face
and my right eye. Wipe
the bloody stuff from my face.

Why did you have to go and deliver roses!
Why? Why did you have to go and deliver
roses. When the Towers
were about to

go

d

o

w

n

d

o

w

n

10/9/01 Tuesday, Tompkins Square Park, almost 12:30,
Loisaida
adios

Rise up
tumble back on the hard dirt.
Fallback, roll down inside
and cry, alone
by the fence. My face kissing the ground—

Why, uncle DJ?

Adios.

Don't say
adios. A thick airy voice
ruffles above me.

Don't say adios yet, Yolanda María.
Pat-pats a handkerchief over my eye.
Wipes my mouth, pat-pats my eye again
and my swollen cheek.

Kisses me nervous and lifts me.
I've been running like Felix Trinidad looking for you.

I heard things outside she tells me.
Mamá stops
suddenly.

Vámonos, she says. Throws the boa
over her shoulder, smoothes Cicatríz's head
and slides her into my backpack.
I hear a little sniff. Sniff.

Mamá lifts me,
almost carries me.

We take the voices now? She asks.
What voices? There's no voices.

The ones you've been carrying
in your backpackah, she says.
How did you know?
I overheard you and Rezzy talking
at Sister Lopez's. I am sorry. So many people
come to her. They want to talk to the *espíritus*
of their loved ones. I was hiding
in one of the dressing rooms.
I didn't know what to say. I've never known
what to say all my life . . .

maybe the voices need to rest, Canelita,
you've carried them a long way.

Mamá and I open the baggies of dust.
One by one, we pour them on the grass,
in a circle around a broken tree, thirsty and bitten.

A tiny feather, a shredded breath
bluish and bright
it spins up and turns above me,
falls to me. I follow its flight
over the busted fence. There it is.

Alone, without a wing, or a body,
incomplete and yet, still alive.

this is the beginning I wanted

Before I open the door
coming home,
Mamá slides off the boa, says
I need to tell you a *secreto*, Yolanda María.
You are tired and hurt, I know.
Your eye, it looks so—Mamá stops
and backs off. Leans against the wall, sobs.
What secret? Mamá?

You know, when I found you this morning
and you prayed out loud for your uncle
and you said adios, adios, adios
over and over again? I wanted to stop you
and tell you that . . .

Uncle DJ?

I wanted to stop, nena
and tell you that—he's home.
Canelita!

A thin but husky voice pulls me into
the Everything Room. Uncle DJ?

I don't know how. Mamá says.
It was you, I think. It was all of us, filling
up our heart with hope and *canciones*
and *velas* in the room and even *merengues*
in the hospital, it was all that. It was
you, Canelita. It was . . .

Uncle DJ?
Sí, corazón. Where you been?
¡Oye, fíjate! You look as bad as me!
How do you like this bed? Folds like a pretzel,
remote control and everything. The mayor
said it's on the house, *cheverote*, eh?

Canelita, come here, you look
like a little wet mouse suckin' a purple
lollipop through your eye.
Uncle DJ?

I open my arms as if falling
into the deep. Down, down,

so far down I cannot see.
But it is me, I know it's me
hugging uncle DJ.

Last thing I remember, he says,
was packing flower bouquets into the basket
on my delivery bicycle at Rosie's Roses, like
a second ago with years in between.
Feel like I was in a Puertorican Purgatory!
Uncle DJ laughs a little, then grabs
tía Gladys's hand and water runs down his eyes.
He lets out a long fluttery breath and
kisses-kisses Tía's hand.

Mamá Mercedes sits
at the foot of her brother's bed.
Touches her heart with her skinny brown hand
as if finally finding it like a lost, torn rose,
a shaky petal that folds everything
back into place.
Tío Beto, I say.
I missed you—so much.
I've been reading your letters

over and over and—
Wait, Mamá! My letters,
my cereal box?

I think you left them at Tompkins
No, you, uh, left them at—

It's all right, chill, says uncle DJ.
Letters? Who needs letters,
when we got each other.
Uncle DJ takes my hand.

Falls
asleep in minutes.

I sit
for a while next to uncle DJ.
Rest my head against the wall.
I notice the IV tubes and the steely chrome
bounce golden
light across the room.
I notice papi Reinaldo sitting on the sofa
clutching his hands together, then
rubbing his face,

maybe he's like me,
he can't believe we are all here again.

Notice
my mother going over uncle DJ's
daily chart of instructions and meds,
she moves like a girl,
with songs and poems
in her little shoulder bones. My legs move
like Mamá's, then I sit by Papi and rest
my head on his shoulder, smells of smoke
and sad air, wind and salt.

I walk up
to the kitchen window
float there—

the sun is still under the avenues, and the
boiling oceans, everything is darkness.

With my hand
over my eye, peek over my city in stacks of black
see my face lit by Mamá's candlelight—

who is she, who was she,
where is she, where was she?

Half of
the face is older,
one eyebrow arches up
asking stuff that cannot be answered,
the puffy lips are curled, with a little smile,
her skin is soft and gauzy,
scratched autumn leaf
and cut, blue
with a rosy reddish meadow
by the forehead, her neck is long
her cheeks are angular,
glowing, still
a little dusty. Now
her lips open almost
about to speak,
it is something inside her
that I notice.
It lights up in places, fiery.
It is a whirlwind,
sparkles wilder—

flies out with a trembling
as if saying

something to life
and blood and dust,
tears and things spinning without
a heart, torn to pieces forever,
crying voices
that never die
and return to our hands, as if
saying it all without one word and
then—

I look at my familia,
before going back to my sofa bed
cradling Cicatríz.

Uncle DJ
wakes up, startled,
smiles, gazes past me,
almost through me.
Hums a little song
as if making up my future.

Gaze at my familia
with soft eyes,

with my eyes made of little rivers, green,
rushing from deep inside, from holy, kind
waters deep-blue-green-green,
where mambos and boleros are born
and girl guitars weep
and burst into islands of fire—

this
is the
beginning I wanted,
Sky.

Cinnamon Words

Abochorrnada como yo: Embarrassed like me

Abuelito: Grandfather

Aguinaldos: Traditional Christmas songs and music

Amor con pastelitos: Love with little banana leaf tamales

Ando esbaratao': I am messed up, falling apart

Apretao': Tight

Arroz: Rice

Asopao': Spicy stew

Bacalaitos: Little fried fish morsels

Bacalao': Dry fish fried

Batey: Patio

¡Bendito!: Holy! Can you believe it?

Bien chévere: Real cool

Bodega: Store

Botica: Drugstore

Buchipluma: A gossip

Cafecito: Little cup of coffee

Caldero: Frying pan

Chéverechévere: Coolcool, great

Chulisnaquis: Beautiful

Cicatríz: Scar

Coctails de camarón: Shrimp cocktails

El cambio: Change of life, menopause

El desarollo: Puberty

Güagüancos: Upbeat Afro-Caribbean drum rhythms

Güapa: Real cute girl

Güapo: Handsome boy

Guayabita: Term of endearment; little guayaba fruit

Habichuelas: Kidney beans

Islita: Little Island, Puerto Rico

Jevos: Tough dudes; "heavies"

La vida es un sueño: From "Life Is a Dream," a famous
    poem by Pedro Calderón de la Barca (1600–1681)

La vida no es un güame: Life ain't peachy, it isn't easy

Lágrimas: Tears

Leche: Milk

Lechón: Roast pork

Loisaida: Lower East Side

Lonche: Lunch

¡Madre Santisima!: Holy Mother of God!

Manguita: Term of endearment; little mango

Me salían granos de antojo en los labios: I used to get
pimples of desire on my lips

Melao': Sugar; sweet substance of sugarcane

Mi Canelita: My little cinnamon stick

Nada: Nothing

Ñaquiti-ñaquiti: Yakkkity yak, talk-talk

Nena: Darling; term of endearment

Noba Yor: New York

Nosedonde: Idon'tknowwhere

Oye, fíjate: Listen, can you believe it?

Palma: Palm leaf

Pantalones: Pants

Paquetero: Schemer, liar

Parranda: House-to-house pilgrimage of Christmas songs

Pasteles: Puerto Rican tamales wrapped in banana leaf

Pellizcos: Pinches

Pescao' frito: Fried fish

Pirulí: Hard candy umbrella-shaped lollipop

Plátanos: Bananas

Pollo frito con habichuelas: Fried chicken with beans

Pueltorras: Puerto Rican women

Puras malas amistades: Just bad friends

Puro bochinche: All gossip and tomfoolery

Puro tumbao': A drum groove; soulful

¿Que te pasa, muchacha?: What's the matter with you, girl?

Quiensabedonde: Whoknowswhere

Ruda: Medicinal rue plant

Sóbame con alcohol: Rub me with alcohol

Sofrito: Fried mix of onions, garlic and cilantro

Té de yerba buena: Spearmint tea

Tendedero: Clothesline

Tengo hoflash: I get the hot flashes; menopause

Timbales: Latin percussion drums

Tostones: Fried bananas

Tráeme el mentolato: Bring me the mentholatum, Vicks

Tripas: Guts

Trulla: Traditional Puerto Rican birthday fiesta

Un flete: An apartment floor; a flat

Vámonos pues: Let's go!

Velas, veladoras: Candles

Venga aquí mi güapa: Come here, my beautiful

Wula: Really; improvised word

Acknowledgments

For Felipe Emilio Herrera and Luz Quintana, my parents, in memory
Margarita Luna Robles, my soul partner, for her love, poetry and art

I would like to thank all my angels:

Joanna Cotler, my publisher, for giving me an open road
Justin Chanda, my editor, for showing me the way
Kendra Marcus, my agent, for asking me to be patient
Harriet Rohmer, for asking me to write for children
Marlene René Segura, my stepdaughter, for introducing me to Sky
Dearly Amara, my student, for her stories
Marvin Bell and Gerald Stern, for the poetry instruments
Ina Cumpiano and Gladys O'Brian, for language and editing
suggestions
Alicia Mikles, for the colors and styles

For Almasol, Joaquín, Joshua, Marlene and Robert—my children
Jeremiah, Rainsong, Ethan and Isabella Yazmin—my grandchildren
For George Robles and Harold Kirkpatrick,
for always having a place for me
Klarissa, JR, BJ, Junior Melendez, Yvette, Catherine, Frankie,
Emilio, Becky, Michael and Nicole, nieces and nephews.
Pilo and Gloria Herrera and my long lost Herrera family.
"Albina's Kids," my great Quintana cousins,
for the early San Francisco days.

For Gloria E. Anzaldúa, Lalo Delgado, Ricardo Aguilar-
Melantzon, RIP.

And for Puerto Rico, our dear 9/11 families, New York City—
for all your endurance, compassion and spirit.